Bully

PRAISE FOR *STORYSHARES*

"One of the brightest innovators and game-changers in the education industry."
– Forbes

"Your success in applying research-validated practices to promote literacy serves as a valuable model for other organizations seeking to create evidence-based literacy programs."

- Library of Congress

"We need powerful social and educational innovation, and Storyshares is breaking new ground. The organization addresses critical problems facing our students and teachers. I am excited about the strategies it brings to the collective work of making sure every student has an equal chance in life."
– Teach For America

"Around the world, this is one of the up-and-coming trailblazers changing the landscape of literacy and education."
- International Literacy Association

"It's the perfect idea. There's really nothing like this. I mean wow, this will be a wonderful experience for young people."   - Andrea Davis Pinkney, Executive Director, Scholastic

"Reading for meaning opens opportunities for a lifetime of learning. Providing emerging readers with engaging texts that are designed to offer both challenges and support for each individual will improve their lives for years to come. Storyshares is a wonderful start."
- David Rose, Co-founder of CAST & UDL

Bully

Tiffany Jones

STORYSHARES

Story Share, Inc.
New York. Boston. Philadelphia

Storyshares
Story Share, Inc.
24 N. Bryn Mawr Avenue #340
Bryn Mawr, PA 19010-3304
www.storyshares.org

Inspiring reading with a new kind of book.

Interest Level: Middle School
Grade Level Equivalent: 3.7

9781973454465

Book design by Storyshares

Printed in the United States of America

Storyshares Presents

1

Holly stepped off the stuffy school bus into the cool spring air. As always, she was wearing her armor. It was invisible, but everyone knew it was there, even the teachers. The sea of students parted as she walked down the school walkway. It made her feel important and lonely at the same time. The feeling was one she had grown used to over the years. Holly converted the feeling to fuel as she entered the building.

Spring break was over, leaving less than half of her sophomore year ahead. For the most part, she had spent the break alone. Holly had no idea what anyone at school had done on vacation. She guessed there was plenty of hanging out with friends. It was something she didn't dwell on. There was no reason to.

Up ahead, obviously in her own little world, was her first target. Blonde, bouncy curls spilled over a pink backpack. She got closer, and spotted a charm bracelet sparkling on a thin wrist. The halls were almost empty since the first bell had rung.

The curly blonde had on clean white canvas sneakers and they called out to Holly. She grinned a wicked grin that made her look a bit crazy. She was just a few feet behind the blonde girl now. The faint smell of strawberries, probably the girl's shampoo, filled the hall.

Holly took a giant step. The toe of her boot slid down the girl's heel, causing her shoe to come loose. Before the girl could react, Holly did it again to the other shoe. The pretty white sneakers were now like flip-flops. As an added bonus, there were black smudges on the backs.

The girl whirled around and Holly saw anger on her face. Almost immediately, the anger turned to a look of indifference. Holly knew it was really a mask for fear.

"What?" Holly asked, with mock innocence.

The girl's cheeks flushed red.

Mrs. Woods was standing in the doorway of her classroom, watching them. Holly scolded herself for not noticing, for being careless. She walked with her head down to the end of the hall. She slipped out the door, knowing the teacher wouldn't follow. She stood on the step outside and studied her boots in the sunlight. The second bell rang and she knew she'd be late to class. That was fine.

Mr. Ward said nothing as she strode in, taking her seat in back. Holly knew he would mark her tardy, but didn't care. She could do whatever algebra problems he assigned, no sweat. She could have gotten As, but chose to fly under the radar. Cs were good enough and didn't come with the risk of attention.

Mr. Ward, like all the other teachers, had learned Holly's code. Leave her alone and she would make things easy during class. Don't dare call her by her given name. Don't dare call on her at all. Adults could be controlled almost as easily as teenagers, Holly had learned.

She bent her head as she worked. Her long brown hair created a curtain that kept the world out. Math calmed her mind because it made perfect sense. The numbers she wrote were small and neat.

After math came World History with Mrs. Woods. If she had seen the game Holly had played that morning, she didn't say a word, just as Holly predicted. She stared down at her dirty fingernails as the teacher droned on.

After History came Spanish, and after Spanish came lunch. She began to strategize. She reminded herself it was better to be feared and respected than liked.

She saw an empty table and made a beeline for it. The table was in a corner. Perfect. Holly set her tray down and began to eat the bland food. She checked her phone while she ate. No one spoke to her, which was just the way she liked it.

The tension slowly began to drain from her body.

Then a voice ruined everything. "Look, it's Holland," the voice said. It was a boy.

Her blood began to boil. She made no move to look at him. She had almost made it through lunch. Almost.

"Big as a country," another voice answered. This one was higher pitched and clearly belonged to a follower.

The leader spoke again. "She doesn't look like she's from Holland at all."

Holly willed herself to stay silent, knowing that in ten minutes she'd be headed to class. From the corner of her eye she saw the two boys leave.

They had on team jackets with varsity letters, and they were laughing at her. Their words dug under her skin like a disease. The sickness was contagious and would soon be passed on.

2

Most people didn't know this, but Holland wasn't actually a country. It was a region on the western coast of the Netherlands.

To Holly, it was the stupidest name in the world to give a person. Her mother claimed to have plucked it out of thin air. That fact made it seem all the more ridiculous. Their ancestors had come from just about everywhere *except* the Netherlands.

Holly slung her black backpack over her shoulder as the school bus stopped. She slid out of her seat and headed down the narrow aisle. Unable to resist, she elbowed the buzz-cut head of a freshman. He started to say something, but saw her and changed his mind.

The day had turned overcast. The chilly air felt damp. Holly hugged herself as she walked the three blocks home.

"Hey, Hol," her mother sang when she heard the front door close.

"Hey," Holly answered.

Her mom asked the usual questions. She responded with "Yeahs" and "Fines" and "Uh-huhs." She grabbed some peanut butter crackers and a can of soda.

"Going to study," she said.

Her mother never talked to Holly about her lack of friends. That silence was a big nothing that took up lots of space. Holly hated the nothing.

It hadn't always been that way. In elementary school, she'd had two best friends, Emma and Sydney. But everything fell apart in middle school. Emma and Sydney went to Avalon, while Holly was zoned for Denton.

Denton Middle School might as well have been another planet. She didn't know a single person there.

At first she felt lonely. Her loneliness turned into self-consciousness, and it seemed like everyone in the school could see it. That was when the teasing started. Sixth grade was like hell on Earth.

By seventh, things had changed. Holly learned to use her anger as a weapon. She became the angry loner. It was much better than her previous character, the scared target.

She got in trouble a few times during her last year at Denton, but managed to talk her way out of it with her mother. It seemed easier for her mom to believe that Holly was just unlucky.

Part of her had wanted her mother's help. Most of her was ashamed and felt like a disappointment. The woman who had named her Holland seemed to be happier not facing the truth.

She brushed cracker crumbs off her shirt and flopped on the bed. She could barely remember her dad's face. He had been out of the picture since she was three. That was another subject her mother never spoke of. Now that Holly was fifteen, she told herself it hardly mattered.

She started to doze in the darkening room. Her mom tapped on the door and she jolted awake.

"Time to eat," her mom said.

Dinner, shower, and bed. She went through the motions without feeling anything.

3

The next morning at her bus stop, she spotted a cricket. As she watched it struggle through the grass, something caught the sunlight. It was a tiny flash, a dewdrop maybe, but she was curious.

She bent down close to see. She heard the bus approaching as she reached into the grass.

The flash had come from a small metal ring. She hid it in her fist. She could feel its grittiness as she settled into the empty seat.

Since April had arrived, warmer weather was finally hinting at an appearance. As she looked out the grimy bus window, the morning suddenly struck her as storybook beautiful.

She nearly dropped her secret prize when she thought she felt it squirm in her hand. Then she looked around to make sure no one had seen.

The ring was partially covered with dirt. It had bumps, possibly gems. Technically, it had been sitting in somebody's yard, but she was pretty sure the spot where she found it was considered public property.

She raised her hand for a bathroom pass during first period and rinsed the ring clean. She tried to slip it over her ring finger but it was too tight. Holly soaped her left hand and tried again. It wasn't easy to get it past the knuckle, but then the silver ring settled in.

She looked at the little heart against her skin. A wave of sickness rolled over her. Heart-shaped jewelry had no place in her life. With the liquid soap still slick on her skin, she pulled. No matter how she twisted and turned it though, the ring wouldn't come off. Soon her finger was bright red from her efforts.

"Never mind," she muttered, and rinsed her hands.

A girl from her class walked in. Seeing Holly at the sink, she started to turn her face away, but without doing it on purpose, Holly felt the corners of her mouth turn up.

The girl (her name was Tina, Holly thought) returned an awkward smile before entering a stall.

Holly looked into the mirror above the sink and saw her smiling reflection. She pushed on her cheeks with her hands, but couldn't make the smile go away. *What was going on?*

She tried to look bored. When Tina came out of the stall, she tried her hardest to scowl.

"Stare a little harder, why don't you," Holly said.

Tina quickly dried her hands, her eyes on the floor. She hadn't been staring at all and Holly knew that. Her words sounded empty in her own ears. She almost felt bad for saying them. Pushing these strange feelings aside, she headed back to class.

Mr. Ward said, "Welcome back," as she walked in.

"Thanks," Holly said softly as she passed.

At her desk, she closed off the world with her hair, as usual. She hadn't planned on answering Mr. Ward. *Was it possible that something was happening inside her?* She remembered her mom saying that hormones caused chemical changes in the brain.

Holly vowed to lay low the rest of the day. She wasn't sure she trusted herself any more.

The ring distracted her all morning. She hid her hands under the desk. The ring finger felt hot, probably from all the tugging.

4

Holly was hungry, but she decided the library was safer than the cafeteria. It was all but deserted. She lost herself in the rows of books. Pulling out a giant atlas, she sat down on the floor.

The maps made her feel small, but somehow powerful. For the first time, Holly wondered if she could change her situation. Something inside her rebelled against the thought. If she changed her behavior, that would mean admitting it needed changing.

She leaned back and rested her head against the metal shelf. She wasn't willing to go there, not yet. Maybe not ever.

By the time she got home, Holly was drained. Her mother was squatting down, yanking weeds from the flowerbed.

"I had to take in some of this beautiful sunshine," her mom said. "After a day like I had, I needed some stress relief."

Holly's mother worked at the hospital as a nurse. Suddenly, Holly was struck with compassion for her. There were crinkles in the corners of her mom's eyes. She worked so hard.

Black soil clung to her mom's hands, reminding Holly of the ring. She turned it around on her finger.

"You okay, Hol?"

"Oh, I'm fine," she said and hurried inside. At least she hadn't said anything weird.

But motherly instinct was making a rare appearance.

"Are you not feeling good?"

Her mom had followed her into the house, and her voice was laced with worry. She wiped her hands on a rag.

Holly tossed her backpack in the corner of the foyer. "I'm just tired, Mom." Horrified, she felt her voice break. *Was she going to cry?*

"Please talk to me," her mom said, and touched her arm.

That small touch was enough to undo her. Holly collapsed onto the couch, her chest heaving with sobs. Her mother rushed over and knelt in front of her.

"What in the world is going on?" she asked.

"Nothing," Holly gasped, and then said, "Everything. It's just... everything."

Her mother rubbed her back, and looked as if she wanted to cry herself. "Did someone hurt you?"

"No, Mom, nothing like that," Holly said. She had no idea how to explain what was happening to her. "You wouldn't get it. Nobody gets it."

"Are you fighting with somebody?"

"What? Who would I be fighting with?" Holly asked, looking her mom in the eyes.

"There was a girl you used to talk with on the phone. What was her name?"

"Do you mean Jessica? That was months ago. We only talked because we were working together on a science project. And guess what, Mom? The teacher chose the partners."

"Is this about a boy?"

Under different circumstances, Holly might have laughed. In her boots, she stood at five foot eleven. Her shoulders were broader than most of the boys' at school. Add the nasty attitude and you got instant boyfriend repellent. She'd found herself crushing on a boy the year before but she she hid it well and waited for the yearning to go away. Any need for friendship was buried and left to die.

"I think I'm sick," she said.

Once the words were out, she realized they gave her an advantage.

At dinner she made a point to leave half her food uneaten. Her mom shot her worried glances across the table. After showering, she shuffled around in her pajamas, trying to look pitiful.

Her mom finally took the bait. "Maybe you ought to stay home tomorrow," she said.

Holly gave herself an inner high five.

Before heading to work the next morning, her mother tiptoed into Holly's room. Her daughter was still wrapped in her blanket and snoring softly.

"Feel better, sweetie," she whispered.

Holly stirred but didn't wake. The soothing words gently broke into her dreams. Her left ring finger pulsed softly.

Bully

5

A little after nine, she finally crawled out of bed. Although Holly wasn't sick, she definitely didn't feel like her normal self. There was something she was now sure of.

The silver ring was changing her. It made no sense, but it was undeniable.

And the ring was impossible to remove. She tried baby oil, butter, even spit. The knuckle seemed to be fighting against her, holding the ring in place.

Giving up, she decided to at least try enjoying her day. It wasn't often that she got to stay home from school. As much as she hated being there, she knew her mom wouldn't put up with too many missed days. She had thought of skipping, but had nowhere to go. Instead, she made life horrible for the people around her.

Suddenly, she saw how she had used her pain to hurt others. Tears welled up in her eyes.

"Stop it!" she shouted into the empty house.

She made pancakes and doused them in syrup before devouring them. She popped popcorn and watched talk shows. She searched the internet for funny videos. Anything to avoid thinking, or feeling.

At noon, she dressed and walked out to the front yard.

The sky was impossibly blue, even more beautiful than yesterday's had been. Holly let the warmth of the sun wash over her.

She had never used a weapon or made anyone bleed. She reminded herself that there were people who'd done worse than she had. None of that mattered, though, and deep down she knew it.

The next thing she knew, she was walking. Her legs were taking her to an unknown destination. The ring was buzzing on her finger.

A few minutes later, she was standing at her bus stop.

She faced the little house. Something seemed to be pulling her up the long walkway, all the way to the front door.

She paused before knocking. It took all her strength.

"What am I going to say?" she thought.

It didn't matter. The ring was in control.

She knocked on the door. A worn-looking woman answered a few moments later. Her eyes were full of both kindness and deep sadness.

"Hello there, young lady," she said.

It seemed as if she had been expecting Holly. No cookies and milk were offered, just a soft, inviting chair.

"I've seen you so many times, I feel like we're already friends," the woman said. A small, amused smile played on her lips.

"I'm Holly," she said, feeling awkward at having been noticed.

"My name is Rose. It's nice to meet you."

"I found a ring on your property," Holly blurted. "I thought the right thing to do would be to return it."

She felt out of control. Her words seemed to have popped out of a hiding place. She settled into the fluffy cushions and waited for whatever might happen next.

"May I see it?" the woman asked.

Holly held out her hand.

6

Rose looked closely and carefully at the ring. Her smile faded and the color drained from her face. She turned to look out the window.

"Last time I saw that ring," she said, "was in 1978."

"So you lost it over thirty years ago, and I found it?" Holly asked in disbelief.

"It belonged to my daughter. Her father and I had given it to her as a gift. It was a sixteenth birthday present. She wore it on the same finger you have it on now. It's in remarkable shape. The ring is white gold, not silver. That's why it never tarnished."

"I bet your daughter will be happy to get it back."

Rose studied Holly for a moment. "My daughter is dead. Ida left this world just after her eighteenth birthday."

Holly felt the blood leave her face. She felt like an idiot for saying the wrong thing.

"I'm sorry," she said. "Could I ask what happened to her?"

The ring was quiet now, the curiosity Holly's alone.

"Well, it isn't a very nice story," Rose said. "I haven't told it in years. But something tells me you should hear it. She was our only child. I'd be lying if I said she wasn't just a bit spoiled. But she was good. I don't mean just ordinarily good, I mean she was especially kind. She thought she could fix the world, and she often tried."

Rose sat down on the couch across from Holly. The framed photo of little Ida sat on the table next to her. She seemed to be watching her mother, listening.

"She met a boy named Walter when she was seventeen. I looked through her eyes and knew what she saw in him. The strong arms, the dark, mysterious eyes. He was a couple years older than Ida. But something wasn't right. A mother knows."

"He thought he was funny. He used to call my girl Idaho Potato. She didn't like it, but didn't want to say so. I knew right then that he had a mean streak. And I was right. He turned out to be a bully."

The word sent chills through Holly, made her want to hide. She thought of telling Rose her real name and how people mocked it. She remained silent instead.

"She moved out on the day she turned eighteen. Walter had a rented room across town. Her father was just sick about it, but he helped her load boxes into Walter's truck anyway. When they were finished, Ida realized the ring had slipped off her finger. She had grown thinner by then. I guess it was lovesickness or stress. Maybe both."

Rose opened a drawer beneath the table and pulled out a photograph. She reached across and handed it to Holly.

"This is the last picture taken of her."

Holly studied it. Even though Ida was wearing sunglasses in the picture, Holly knew there was pain in her eyes. It was a pain that would remain forever hidden.

"She's pretty," was all Holly could manage.

"She was beautiful," Rose agreed, "inside and out."

Holly returned the picture and Rose set it on the table.

"It was almost dark by then. My husband got us a couple flashlights and we looked all over the yard, but couldn't find the ring. Walter sat in his truck, I'll never forget it. He just tapped his thumb on the steering wheel until Ida gave up looking."

"Once that truck tore out of the driveway, I never saw Ida again. It's hard to believe, but she'd be in her fifties now. In my mind, she's still just a child. She never got the chance to be a mother, to make me a grandma."

Rose looked at her hands folded in her lap. Holly's heart was pounding, afraid to hear what happened to Ida.

"I'll spare you the details," Rose said softly, as if reading her mind. "Walter was found guilty of killing Ida. He died in prison about ten years ago."

Holly felt a tickle on her cheek and realized she was crying.

"There were bruises," Rose said dreamily, "but she always explained them away."

"I'm so sorry," Holly whispered.

"Since my husband passed last year, I've been alone. I try to keep busy with volunteer work. I try to help others. It's what Ida would have wanted. I forgave Walter a long time ago. Some people didn't understand that, but I had figured something out."

She stopped. Holly had to ask. "What had you figured out?"

"I felt so empty after she was gone. Then guilt filled the emptiness. Why hadn't I done more? I became angry, too. These feelings were normal, but they were changing me. I was becoming so negative, so hateful. I had to forgive

Walter so I could get free of the hate and anger. If I became a good person again, in that way, Ida could live on."

Holly understood what it felt like to be a negative force. She looked down at the ring and spun it one full revolution. Not expecting much, she pulled, and to her surprise it slid right off.

She handed it to Rose, and Rose slid it over the bony knuckle of her left pinky finger.

"I can feel her," Rose said, placing her hand over her heart. "I can feel my Ida." A joyous smile spread across her face.

Holly knew exactly what she meant.

7

Holly walked over to the window. She stared down at her bus stop, imagining Rose seeing her there. She saw an image of herself: dark clothes, head down, hating the world.

"Are you all right?" Rose asked gently.

Holly turned around and saw the worried look on Rose's face. She felt a crumbling of something tough inside her.

"Ida's ring..." Holly began. But she didn't know what else to say.

"...Is the reason we are talking right now," Rose said. "It has worked a kind of magic, hasn't it?"

"More than you know," Holly replied. "It did something to me. It made me feel good, made me want to *be* good. I know that must sound really stupid. It's just that... I've been an awful person, Rose. You have no idea."

Holly hung her head, letting her tears fall to the floor. She felt the weight of all the time she had wasted. And here was Rose, after all she had been through, reaching out. She had had everything taken from her and she was still giving.

"The ring may have nudged you in the right direction," Rose said. "But the good was already in you. We all make mistakes, Holly. It's never too late to change."

"How do you do it? How can you want to help other people after you were hurt so bad?" Holly asked.

"Come sit down," Rose said, patting the couch cushion next to her.

Holly sat and Rose took her hand. She could once again feel the ring against her skin. The tears were still flowing from her eyes. All the pain she had been holding inside was finally being released. Hope was taking its place.

"You've already begun doing good, don't you see? This has been such a wondrous day for me. Ida's ring came back to me. And I finally got to meet you."

"You wanted to meet me?" Holly asked in disbelief. "Why?"

"You're strong," Rose said. "I could see that from my window. You looked like a diamond in the rough, and I see I was right. Those are the best kinds of friends to have, you know."

Holly didn't feel like a diamond, not even in the rough. The possibility of friendship though, was like remembering a forgotten dream.

"I wonder... Would you like to come help me at the food pantry tomorrow?" Rose asked. "I volunteer there every Thursday afternoon from three until five."

"Sure," Holly said quickly, "that would be awesome."

"You should check with your mother first. If she doesn't mind, just come on up after the bus drops you off."

"My mother!" Holly exclaimed, pulling her phone out. It was after two, and her mom would be home soon. "I have to go. But I'll see you tomorrow."

"I'm looking forward to it," Rose said. She stood and hugged Holly, her thin arms squeezing tight.

"Thank you so much," Holly said softly. "You have no idea..."

"I think I do," Rose answered. She pulled away and held Holly's shoulders, looking her in the eyes. "I know exactly what you mean."

Rose walked Holly to the door and closed it softly behind her. Holly headed down the walkway and towards home.

She felt physically lighter somehow, as new as the creations of spring. Change was all around her, blossoming inside her.

She looked at her finger, the brief and former home of Ida's ring. It had left a faint, heart-shaped impression on her skin. Holly knew it would soon fade, but that was okay. She didn't need to see the heart to know it was real.

About The Author

Tiffany Jones lives in Central Florida with her husband and two daughters. Writing is her passion and she hopes to one day have one of her novels published. The Story Shares Contest gave her the opportunity to write a story that she hopes will be an inspiration to others.

About The Publisher

Story Shares is a nonprofit focused on supporting the millions of teens and adults who struggle with reading by creating a new shelf in the library specifically for them. The ever-growing collection features content that is compelling and culturally relevant for teens and adults, yet still readable at a range of lower reading levels.

Story Shares generates content by engaging deeply with writers, bringing together a community to create this new kind of book. With more intriguing and approachable stories to choose from, the teens and adults who have fallen behind are improving their skills and beginning to discover the joy of reading. For more information, visit storyshares.org.

Easy to Read. Hard to Put Down.

www.ingramcontent.com/pod-product-compliance
Lightning Source LLC
Chambersburg PA
CBHW071228170626
46809CB00005BA/1974